# COVENTRY LIBRARIES

Please return this book on or before
the last date stamped below.

To renew any items:

Coventry City Council

- visit any Coventry Library
- go online to www.coventry.gov.uk/libraries
- telephone 024 7683 1999

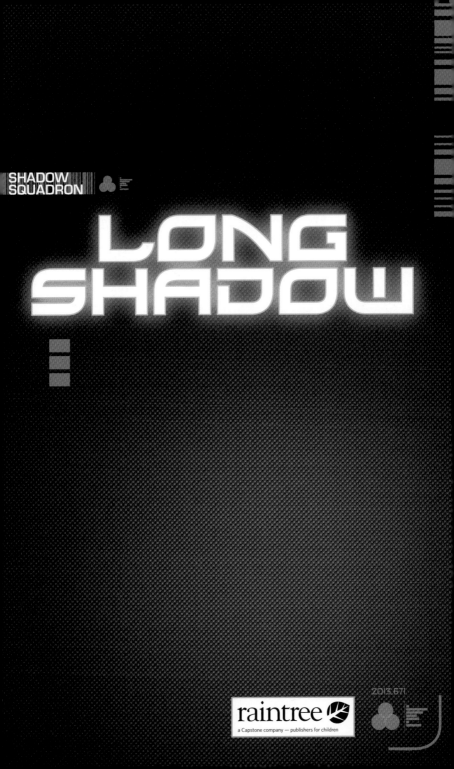

SHADOW
SQUADRON

# LONG
# SHADOW

raintree
a Capstone company — publishers for children

SHADOW
SQUADRON

# LONG
# SHADOW

WRITTEN BY
CARL BOWEN

ILLUSTRATED BY
WILSON TORTOSA

AND
BENNY FUENTES

COVER ART BY
MARC LEE

2012.241

*AUTHORIZING*

Raintree is an imprint of Capstone Global Library
Limited, a company incorporated in England and
Wales having its registered office at 7 Pilgrim
Street, London, EC4V 6LB – Registered company
number: 6695582

www.raintree.co.uk
myorders@raintree.co.uk

First published by Stone Arch Books © 2015
First published in the United Kingdom in 2015

ISBN: 978-1-4747-0543-1 (paperback)
ISBN: 978-1-4747-0548-6 (eBook PDF)

British Library Cataloguing in Publication Data

A full catalogue record for this book is available
from the British Library.

Printed in China

# CONTENTS

1316.981

2012.101

ACCESS GRANTED

## SHADOW SQUADRON DOSSIER

### CROSS, RYAN

RANK: Lieutenant Commander
BRANCH: Navy Seal
PSYCH PROFILE: Cross is the team leader of Shadow Squadron. Control oriented and loyal, Cross insisted on hand-picking each member of his squad.

### PAXTON, ADAM

RANK: Sergeant First Class
BRANCH: Army (Green Beret)
PSYCH PROFILE: Paxton has a knack for filling the role most needed in any team. His loyalty makes him a born second-in-command.

PHOTO NOT AVAILABLE

IZI6.06Z

### YAMASHITA, KIMIYO

RANK: Lieutenant
BRANCH: Army Ranger
PSYCH PROFILE: The team's sniper is an expert marksman and a true stoic. It seems his emotions are as steady as his trigger finger.

## LANCASTER, MORGAN

RANK: Staff Sergeant
BRANCH: Air Force Combat Control
PSYCH PROFILE: The team's newest member is a tech expert who learns fast and has the ability to adapt to any combat situation.

PHOTO NOT AVAILABLE

## JANNATI, ARAM

RANK: Second Lieutenant
BRANCH: Army Ranger
PSYCH PROFILE: Jannati serves as the team's linguist. His sharp eyes serve him well as a spotter, and he's usually paired with Yamashita on overwatch.

PHOTO NOT AVAILABLE

## SHEPHERD, MARK

RANK: Lieutenant
BRANCH: Army (Green Beret)
PSYCH PROFILE: The heavy-weapons expert of the group, Shepherd's love of combat borders on unhealthy.

2019.681

## MISSION BRIEFING

OPERATION

### LONG SHADOW 011

We've received video footage of a terrorist claiming responsibility for some heinous acts. It's more of a propaganda piece intended to rally the terrorist troops, but despite that, the JSOC wants answers. We've therefore been tasked with dropping in, grabbing the terrorist, and getting him out alive.

Getting in will be easy, but we'll have to get creative with the exfiltration.

– Lieutenant Commander Ryan Cross

3245.98 ● ● ●

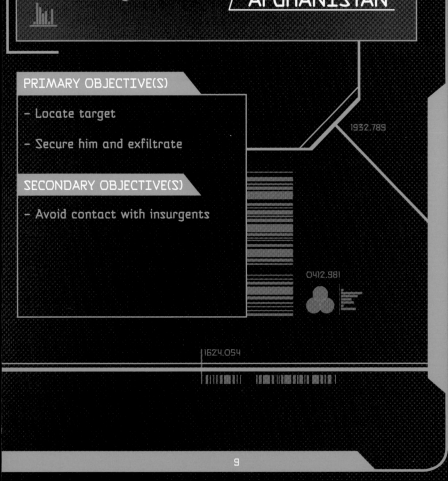

# AFGHANISTAN

## PRIMARY OBJECTIVE(S)

- Locate target

- Secure him and exfiltrate

## SECONDARY OBJECTIVE(S)

- Avoid contact with insurgents

1932.789

0412.981

1624.054

## INTEL

*DECRYPTING*

12345

## COM CHATTER

- KA-BAR: utility knife sometimes used in combat
- MH-53J: long-range combat and rescue helicopter
- PSY-OPS: psychological operations used to manipulate the minds of enemies

3245.98 ● ● ●

# INCEPTION

*Nine years ago…*

One minute the MH-53J helicopter's cabin was tense and almost silent, the air thick with anticipation. The only sounds were the chopping thrum of the engine and the low grumbling conversations of soldiers preparing for bitter business in hostile territory. The next minute, a thunderous explosion tore the world apart, hurling the soldiers into a nightmare from which most would never wake.

## KABOOM!

The world spun as the soldiers tumbled around the cramped interior of the helicopter. Alarms yowled like injured animals. A dozen voices overlapped each other, making it impossible to tell who was shouting or what they were saying.

The only voice Chief Petty Officer Alonso Walker could make out was the pilot alternately cursing and praying as he fought to keep his bird in the air – and his passengers alive. Walker focused on that one voice. He blocked out all the panic, anger, adrenaline-fuelled insanity and the unexpectedly child-like terror.

Like the rest of them, Walker knew the chopper was going down. There was nothing anyone could do about it.

## BOOM!

A secondary explosion from the rear kicked the helicopter around in the other direction, setting the rear cabin on fire and ripping the tail off.

Through a ring of flames and billowing smoke, Walker saw nothing but hints of rocky canyon walls getting ever closer.

Then the black, starless sky closed in on him.

* * *

The acrid burn of smoke in the back of Walker's throat awoke him. He didn't know how much time had passed. He tried to cough out the smoke, but it was everywhere, blinding and suffocating him.

*"Chief..."*

Something lay on top of him. It dug into the bottom of his ribs and made it hard to breathe. His right arm was twisted in a Gordian knot of tangled harness straps. When he tried to free himself, white-hot pain exploded in his shoulder.

He'd dislocated the same shoulder several times while playing football in high school. It had never hurt this much before.

*"Chief..."*

His left arm was pinned beneath his body, but

he managed to wiggle it free. Somehow he managed to lift whatever it was that lay across his chest. His trembling fingers felt Kevlar body armour sticky with drying blood.

*One of the men,* he realized.

He couldn't tell who it was through all the smoke. All he could do was follow the arm to the wrist.

*No pulse,* he realized.

With an awkward left-handed push that made his shoulder burn with agony, he shoved the dead man off him. Now he could breathe, but that just let the smoke in more easily.

*"Chief."*

Walker held his breath and listened, trying not to cough or choke on smoke. He could hear the crackle of distant fire but nothing else near by. Then he heard a ragged, hissing whimper like the sound of an animal in awful pain.

It took him a few moments to realize that the noise was coming from his own mouth.

*"Chief!"*

The fact that his mind felt disconnected from that pain was a mixed blessing. It was likely that he was going into shock. Or paralyzed. Or dying.

*And why does my shoulder hurt so much?* he wondered.

*"CHIEF!"*

Walker's eyes opened again. He'd come dangerously close to passing out. Now the smoke was thin enough to see through. He saw the new team member coming towards him, the medic. The team's little brother and mascot. The medic hated how the others treated him like a child. Walker was the only one who showed him respect.

"There you are, Chief!" the medic said. "Thank goodness you're alive!"

"Medic..." Walker coughed the word out. He struggled over to the left with his free hand, trying to touch the soldier who'd been lying on top of him. "Over here. He's got no pulse..."

The medic pushed the dead soldier out of the way

with his boot. He crouched next to the Chief. Walker half expected the young medic to be panicked or frantic, but all he saw was a blank mask of concentration.

The medic gave his head a quick shake to keep the blood from a cut on his forehead out of his eye. "Can you move?" the medic hissed.

Walker realized he must have blacked out. He made an effort to focus. "My arm," he croaked out. "Hand's caught. Shoulder's out. And my back... I think it's broken. Hurts."

"If it hurts, then it's probably not broken," the medic said.

"Smart aleck," Walker croaked.

The medic examined Walker's trapped right arm and moved to that side of him. Shoving a mangled seat out of the way, he found the mass of canvas straps cinched tightly around Walker's wrist. They were cutting off circulation and binding his arm. The medic dug a knuckle into the middle of the knot, trying to loosen it, but that only put more tension on the strap and made Walker cry out in pain.

A breeze pushed more smoke in on the two of them, making them cough and flail until the wind shifted. When Walker could see again, the medic was holding an old Ka-Bar knife and looking down at Walker's trapped arm with a grimace.

"I won't lie, Chief," the medic said. "This is going to hurt."

Before the medic had finished, Walker screamed and passed out.

* * *

When Walker came round, he didn't know if it was still night or if daytime had come and gone again. He found himself lying on the hard, rock floor of a small cave. A chemical glow stick provided weak, sickly illumination.

Walker tried to sit up. A throb of pain ran through his right shoulder, but it wasn't anywhere near the intensity it had been before. A moment of panic swept over him as he remembered the last thing he'd seen: the medic trying to cut his hand off with a Ka-Bar blade.

Walker stretched his neck to look at the damage, and his panic turned to confusion. His arm was wrapped tightly in a makeshift sling, and his bruised hand was bandaged. He couldn't make sense of it. Had the medic cut his hand off and then … reattached it somehow?

"Good news," came a familiar voice from across the cave. It wasn't the medic. "Apparently your back's not broken."

"Temple? Is that you?" Walker croaked. His eyes had difficulty focusing, but he managed to make out the face of the team's psy-ops expert.

The Green Beret's eyes were glazed over. He lay propped up on one side, his legs hidden behind him in shadow, staring at nothing in particular. His Kevlar jacket was gone, revealing a thick mummy-wrap of bandages around his torso. The entire left side of his face was covered as well.

"Looks like you got off lightly, Chief," Temple said, wincing with every word. "You shot?"

"I don't think so," Walker said. "You?"

"If only," Temple muttered.

"Am I drugged?" Walker asked.

"A little," Temple said. "You probably slept off the best part. And don't expect more. The kid loaded me up before he left."

Walker could feel clarity seeping back into his mind, bringing with it a thousand dull aches and bone-deep throbs. He also realized why his hand was still there: the medic had cut the straps that his wrist had been trapped in. It was probably just sprained.

"What happened?" the Chief asked, not sure if he wanted to know.

"Stinger missile," Temple said. "Blew our tail off when we dropped into the valley. Shooter was probably hiding in a cave just like this one. Waited for us to fly over, then bang. Little coward was waiting for us."

"How many of us made it?" Walker asked.

"Five that I know of," Temple said. "Well, five plus you. Five total if the kid doesn't come back."

"Who are the other three?" Walker asked.

"The *Rangers*," Temple said, spitting the words out. "Not a scratch between them, if you can believe it. Lucky them."

"Where are they?" Walker asked.

The hate blazing in Temple's eyes was so hot that Walker flinched. "They left us," Temple snarled.

"They wouldn't," Walker said. No soldier with any sense of decency would abandon their team-mates. Especially not the top-tier, elite special ops soldiers the Joint Special Operations Command had pulled together for this programme. "They must not have known anyone else survived."

"They knew, Chief," the medic said as he entered the cave. "They helped me get Temple here and stood guard while I got him patched up. After that, Major Edmonds convinced Whitney and Jacobs that they had to finish the mission. I told them we had to finish looking for survivors and get out of here alive, but he wouldn't hear it."

"Like he said," Temple hissed, clutching his chest with one heavily bandaged hand. "And then Edmonds said that the rest of us were as good as dead anyway, and if the boy here wanted to stay and die too, that was his choice."

"And they just left?" Walker asked in disbelief.

The medic nodded. "The Taliban is combing the area for survivors of the helicopter crash. Edmonds said somebody had to slip through the net before the terrorists caught all of us. The mission has to come first." He paused. A shadow of a scowl crossed his face. "You know what Edmonds is like."

Walker didn't say anything. Although he was technically Major Edmonds's second-in-command, he and the Ranger got along like cats and dogs. Ever since their multi-branch unit had been formed, they never saw eye to eye. Edmonds only truly trusted his fellow Rangers. He tolerated the Green Berets, ignored the two Marines, and openly despised the Air Force and Navy soldiers on his team. The man seemed to think that mixing special operations units was a terrible idea. It was clear to Walker that Edmonds had taken the assignment as a stepping stone to a higher rank.

"So how bad is it?" Walker asked.

"Nobody else has made it," the medic said. "The chopper's a write-off – nothing salvageable. The Taliban were buzzing around it like flies when I went back to it after bringing you here. They put a bullet in every body they found and were getting ready to put one last RPG in what's left of the wreckage. Last I heard, they were fanning out to look for the remaining six of us."

Walker frowned. "They *said* six? Specifically six?"

The medic nodded.

"How did they know how many of us were present?" Walker asked. "For that matter, how did they know where to ambush us in the first place?"

"Does it matter?" Temple snapped. A hideous cough then doubled him over.

"Guess not," the medic said. "What matters is the Taliban is looking for survivors, and they're already all over the valley. We can't afford to stay here."

Temple smirked. "Now tell him the bad news."

"Temple's in bad shape," the medic said. "Broken ribs, shrapnel, third-degree burns on his torso. And his leg is … well, it's broken. Let's leave it at that."

"Now's not the time to get squeamish, kid," Temple said. With a flourish, he heaved his left leg into the light. His boot, sock and trousers were gone. A thick strip of what was left of his trouser leg was tied off tightly above his knee. Everything below it was a mangled mess of flesh and bone. The bandages were already stained reddish yellow.

"Multiple open fractures," the kid said, his voice taking on a distant tone. "Severe crushing injury to the foot. Femoral artery's a wreck. I had to tourniquet the whole leg so he didn't bleed out just getting him here. I'm not exactly qualified to, you know, perform an, um–"

"Just spit it out," Temple said. "I already know what you're going to say."

"He's going to lose the foot," the medic said to Walker. "Maybe everything below the knee. That's assuming we can get him to a hospital. If not, we'll have gangrene to worry about on top of everything else, assuming his burns don't get infected first."

"And my ear's gone," Temple said. "Don't forget that part. My days on the beauty pageant circuit are over."

Temple let out a wild cackle. Walker heard hysteria in the laughter, which quickly turned into a coughing fit.

Walker glanced at the medic for confirmation. The medic caught his glance and nodded. "I gave him all the morphine I had, Chief," the medic said quietly. "I hoped it would be enough to knock him out, but he just won't go down."

"Is there anything else you can do for him here?" Walker asked.

The medic shook his head.

"Then we need to get out of here now," Walker said. His body still ached, but he managed to sit up and pull the sling off his right arm. With his shoulder back in its socket, it was now just sore rather than immobile and useless. His back was in bad shape, but at least nothing was broken. "If we can get outside the Taliban's search area—"

"If you think I'm going anywhere without a heavy dose of morphine, you're out of your mind," Temple said. "And if one of you fools tries to pick me up and carry me, I'm going to knock you out. It was bad enough the first time."

"Moving him's torture," the medic said with a tiny shudder. "And we don't have the morphine to knock him out. We wouldn't be able to move quietly. Tough as he is, there's only so much he can take."

"Nothing personal," Temple said. "It's just that when I'm in incredible pain without the drugs, I get a little scream-y."

"You could go, Chief," the medic said. "Slip out and find Edmonds. Work out what his evacuation plan is, then convince him to come back for us."

"We don't have time for that," Walker said. "The Taliban would find you before I could get back."

"We could surrender," the medic suggested.

"You know who they are," Walker said, cutting through the medic's innocence. "They won't take prisoners. They'll kill us, torture us, or both."

The medic sighed. They really only had one choice, but none of the three men wanted to be the one to say the words.

"You're going to make me say it, aren't you?" Temple asked. He spat out a glob of blood. "Fine, I'll let you cowards off the hook. You two go. Squeak your way out the back like little mice while I crawl out to the front of the cave and lure the bad guys to me. I can keep them in a stalemate here until I'm nobody's problem anymore."

"You don't even have a gun," the medic said.

"Actually, I do," Temple said, reaching behind his back. He produced a Beretta M9 and gave it a little flourish. "Whitney left me his back-up weapon in case things got even worse while you were out looking for more survivors. I can make some noise with it, at least. Draw their focus so you two can escape."

Walker's jaw tightened. He couldn't bring himself

to say that Temple was right. The man was offering to sacrifice himself for their sake even though he clearly didn't want to do it, but it was the only choice they had if any of them hoped to escape. Walker knew this. Temple knew this. But the medic could only shake his head, unwilling to face cold, hard reality.

"Quit your head-wagging, kid – you don't get a say in this," Temple grumbled. "I'm going to give you to the count of five. If you're not gone when I get to five, well…"

Temple placed the gun under his own chin.

"…I'm going to make an ugly mess and a loud noise."

"His mind's made up, son," Walker said to the medic, aggravated that he couldn't think of a better option. "We have to respect his wishes." The medic shook his head "no" again, so Walker looked at Temple and said, "Start counting."

"Four…" Temple said.

"All right, all right," the medic said, his voice sounding as defeated as Walker felt. Without another word, the medic turned and walked out of the cave the way he'd entered.

Walker waited until the kid had left. Then he nodded at Temple and gave him a stiff formal salute. Temple smirked and didn't return the gesture. Walker gave him one last moment to see if the man had any last words.

"Three and a half," was all Temple said.

Walker left.

* * *

*Today...*

Lieutenant Commander Ryan Cross was enjoying a rare liberty: a football game. He was sitting high up on the concrete stadium bleachers of his old high school, watching his team lose at its own homecoming game. The attack was underperforming, and the defence had given up back-to-back touchdowns in the opening minutes of the second quarter. The drubbing brought back fond memories of Cross's days in the marching band, helping to boost the team's morale from the sidelines.

It had just started drizzling – adding insult to injury, really – when the phone in his pocket buzzed with an incoming call. Cross glanced at the display on his smartwatch: *BASE CALLING.*

*So much for relaxation,* Cross thought. He dug his phone out of his pocket. "Cross here," he said.

"It's me, Boss," one of his men said. The voice belonged to Carter Howard, the newest member of his team – on permanent loan from the CIA's Special Activities Division. "Sorry to barge in on your week off, but time is of the essence."

Cross sighed. "When isn't it?" he grumbled. "What's going on?"

"Can't say over the phone," Howard told him. "They'll give you the whole story back at base. There's a taxi on the way to pick you up."

"I doubt that," Cross said. "I haven't even told you where I am."

"Yes, we saw that you turned off your phone's GPS," Carter said. "There's another one in your watch, though."

Cross glanced at the smartwatch again. For a moment, he seriously considered leaving it behind when he left. The only reason he wore the over-priced watch was that a friend and former team-mate had sent it to him for his birthday last year.

"Wise guy," Cross mumbled.

"See you in a few hours, Boss," Carter said.

Cross stood up, trying not to feel bitter about the lost liberty. "On my way."

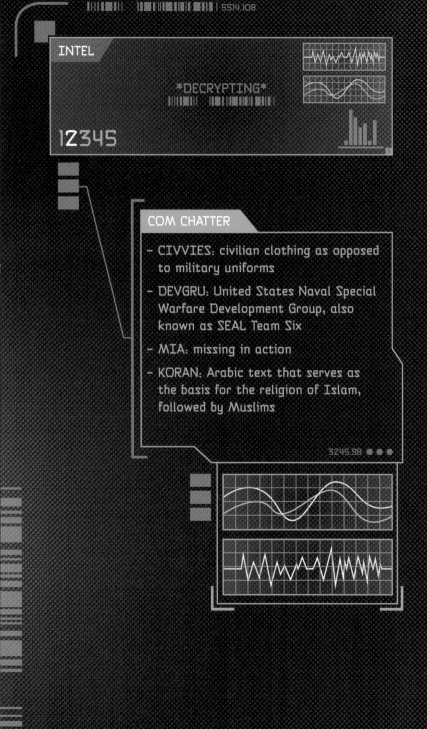

INTEL

*DECRYPTING*

12345

## COM CHATTER

- CIVVIES: civilian clothing as opposed to military uniforms

- DEVGRU: United States Naval Special Warfare Development Group, also known as SEAL Team Six

- MIA: missing in action

- KORAN: Arabic text that serves as the basis for the religion of Islam, followed by Muslims

3245.98

# IMPRESSION

A few months ago, Carter Howard became the newest member of Ryan Cross's top-secret special ops team called Shadow Squadron. The unit – Cross's unit, created especially for him – brought together the best of the elite soldiers from all branches of the military. His squad consisted of members of the Army's Green Berets and Rangers, the Navy SEALs (where Cross proudly hailed), the Marines Special Operations Regiment and Air Force Combat Control.

It was a unique team, to say the least. But under Cross's leadership, the unit had faced threats all over the world, from Somali pirates to Russian Spetznaz to Malian slavers to Colombian drug-smugglers. Wherever the US had an interest in taking military action but couldn't act openly for political, tactical or legal reasons, the Joint Special Operations Command called upon Shadow Squadron. Its mission success rate was exceptional, and its casualty rate was minimal (though each loss had been devastating).

Cross's mind shifted away from his team's losses as he arrived back at base and spotted a familiar van in the car park. With a mix of anticipation and uncharacteristic nervousness, he hurried inside to his quarters, changed out of his civvies, and made his way to his office. There he found the man the van belonged to: his former second-in-command, Chief Petty Officer Alonso Walker (retired).

"Chief!" Cross said, forcing extra enthusiasm into his voice. "This is a surprise. What brings you here?"

Walker was a trim, fit career Navy SEAL in his early 40s. Recommended by Command at the formation of Shadow Squadron for his experience and unfailing professionalism, Walker had proven himself an invaluable asset to the new team. He had

been able to shift between the roles of best friend, stern father and mediator at a moment's notice – whichever role suited the team's needs. He was tough, tactically brilliant and had a gift for languages that Cross envied.

At first, Walker had struggled to accept Cross's leadership. But with a little time and a series of successful missions to his credit, Cross had earned Walker's trust, respect and even friendship.

But now, wearing a tired grin, Walker was restricted to using a wheelchair – and a clunky plastic hearing aid in his right ear.

"Good morning, Ryan," Walker said, just a little bit too loud. "I told you not to call me Chief anymore."

The older SEAL's career with Shadow Squadron had ended a year ago after a mission in Yemen. Hot on the heels of a notorious bomb-maker, the team was betrayed by the corrupt CIA special agent who had set up the mission. That agent, the late Bradley Upton, had organized a bombing to distract and disrupt Shadow Squadron's operation in order to kidnap Cross and try to recruit him into the criminal empire Upton had been building.

Cross refused that offer. Thankfully, the team was able to free him from Upton's clutches, but the bombing had taken its toll. Walker had been paralyzed in the blast, and his hearing had been damaged. He was completely deaf in his left ear and almost deaf in his right. When the mission was over, Command commended Cross as a hero for his bravery and integrity. All Walker had got was early retirement, a full package of benefits and the implied thanks of a grateful nation that would never know anything about everything Walker had done for them.

"I can't help it," Cross said. "It doesn't feel right just calling you 'Walker'."

"Why?" Walker asked with a blank face. "The irony?"

Cross's stomach did a little flip. His mouth opened and closed without making any sound. He couldn't believe he'd been stupid enough to say that.

"What? Chief, no – I mean, Walker, I–" Cross

said. "I just meant it's too casual! I'm so sorry. I didn't mean to–"

Walker let Cross suffer for several long, agonizing moments before breaking into a guffaw that boomed down the hallway.

"I wish you could see your face right now," Walker choked out between chuckles.

Cross shook his head and smiled. He felt like an idiot, but at least he was less nervous than he'd been since he'd first seen Walker's van in the car park. "Why don't we get out of my office and then you can tell me why you're here," he said.

"Sure," Walker said. He effortlessly pivoted his chair in a tight circle with one arm and rolled into the hallway. "Let's take this to the briefing room. Would you like some coffee?"

"I'll get it," Cross said, grinning. "You just concentrate on rolling into a deep ditch and staying there for the rest of your life."

Walker chuckled. "Yessir," he chirped. Still laughing, he wheeled down the hallway.

Cross went the other way, grabbed two cups of coffee – one black, one sweet – then entered the briefing room. The only other member of the team present was Howard, dressed smartly in his tailored Shadow Squadron uniform. He and Walker were chatting amiably as Howard sipped from his own coffee mug.

Cross handed Walker the sweetened cup of coffee. He looked up at the computer whiteboard displaying the sword-and-globe emblem of Joint Special Operations Command. Howard was toying with the touch screen built into the top of the table in the middle of the room.

Howard caught Cross's gaze. "Morning, Boss," he said. "Have a good flight?"

"Long one," Cross mumbled. "So will someone tell me what this is all about? Am I even in charge around here anymore?"

Howard had the good grace to at least look a little embarrassed. "Yes, sorry for all the hush-hush behaviour. I wanted to tell you over the phone or at least send you the video, but Command locked everything down. They don't want it leaving the building."

"But this is something the Chief's cleared to see?" Cross asked.

"Yes, evidently," Howard said, sounding as confused as Cross. Not that the Chief couldn't be trusted, of course, but he was only a civilian now. "Command wanted him as a consultant. Apparently it concerns something he has insight on."

"What is it about?" Cross asked.

Walker only shrugged.

"Command says to watch the video first," Howard said. "They didn't want me to influence your first impression of it."

"What video?" Cross asked, annoyed by the mysterious circumstances. If this was mission-related, Command should have come to him first. The fact that Howard knew more than he did was highly irregular. Then again, having a former CIA operative on his team meant that this sort of thing would happen from time to time. The CIA tended to only trust their own.

Howard tapped the touch screen, replacing the JSOC emblem with a digital video of a scarred white man wearing a black Afghan tunic. He sat in front of a black curtain at a small desk with a blood-red top. A silver calligraphic rendition of the traditional Islamic bismillah was written across the top. Beneath it was a pair of verses from the Koran, one over each of the white man's shoulders.

As the video began, the man at the desk turned a switch on an oil lamp in front of him, casting a sickly glare over his haggard and drawn face. His stringy beard was streaked with grey. A hideous scar mottled the right half of his head, though he tried to keep that side in the shadows. At the sight of him, Walker let out a surprised gasp.

"I am Aswad Sayif," the man said in Arabic. "It is my orders that you follow. You will never see my face or hear my voice again, but know that you are instruments of my will. Your victories are my victories, won in the name of Allah, the Most Gracious, the Most Powerful."

The man continued for several minutes, speaking

of recent bombings and kidnappings and insurgent raids. As he spoke, the video cut to news footage of violent incidents occurring in Afghanistan against civilian and US military targets.

When the man reappeared on the screen, he claimed responsibility for planning and remotely overseeing these acts, then praised the viewers of the video for carrying them out.

Only then did Cross realize that this video wasn't a recorded threat meant to undermine enemy morale – or a misguided call to action addressed to the greater Muslim world. It wasn't a public declaration of Jihad. It was a pep talk from an insurgent leader intended for fellow insurgents' ears only.

The man ended his speech with two verses from the Koran, presumably the ones referenced by the chapter and verse number on the curtain behind him. First he said, "The Koran says, 'Fight and slay the infidels wherever you find them'. It also says, 'God will punish them by your hands and will disgrace them and give you victory over them and satisfy the believers'. Hear now my words, fellow warriors.

If you wish to be the friends of God, gladly do the things which you know will please him."

On that disturbing note, the man in the video dimmed the oil lamp, cloaking his face in shadow once again. A few seconds later, the video stopped. Howard cleared it from the screen then looked at Cross.

"What's your first impression, Boss?" Howard asked.

"Something about it feels off," Cross said. "But I can't quite put my finger on it. I've heard that name before, though. It means 'The Black Sword.' A lot of insurgents claimed to get their orders from a source going by that name. The Afghanis on our side thought it was just a bogeyman. The CIA thought it was a whole group of rogue terrorists trying to coordinate the insurgency from the shadows. My CO thought it was a terrorist code-name for bin Laden. I've never seen or heard any information that confirmed any of it, but the name carried a lot of weight during the war. Is that really him?"

"Sort of," Howard said.

"He's no Afghani," Cross said. "Where'd this video come from?"

"DEVGRU," Howard said, referring to the Navy's Special Warfare Development Group – known in the popular media as SEAL Team Six. "They found a computer with that video on it after a raid on an Al-Qaeda training camp in Pakistan. The survivors confirmed it was sent to them from Aswad Sayif to congratulate them after a successful mission."

"He's American," Walker said with a scowl.

Cross decided that Walker must be able to make this out from subtleties in the man's accent.

Howard nodded. "Anyway, they kicked the computer over to Phantom Cell," Howard continued, referring to a black-tier special operations unit that focused on psychological operations and cyberwarfare. "They analyzed the video and traced it back to its source. Their intel says it came from an insurgent safe house hidden in the Safed Koh mountain range in the Nangahar Province in Afghanistan. They code-named it *Shangri-La*. Apparently they've been looking for it since before bin Laden escaped into Pakistan."

"Sounds straightforward," Cross said. "So how did this come to you first? And what's the Chief's role?"

Howard shrugged. "They wanted his opinion on Aswad Sayif," he said. "That's all they told me."

"That man isn't Aswad Sayif," Walker said, his voice an angry growl. "His name's Gareth Temple. He was a brother in arms – one I thought had been dead for the last nine years."

"What?" Cross asked. "You know this man? He was a SEAL?"

"Service record says Green Beret," Howard said, peering down at the touch screen in the tabletop. "He went MIA in Afghanistan during the war. Presumed killed nine years ago during Operation Long Shadow ... which is apparently classified higher than my level. That's odd."

"I was part of Long Shadow myself," Walker said. He looked at Cross. "That's why they wanted me here. It was the final mission of Shadow Squadron. The *first* Shadow Squadron."

**INTEL**

*DECRYPTING*

12345

**COM CHATTER**

- AL-QAEDA: global militant Islamic
  group known for terrorist acts
- MQ-9 REAPER: unmanned aerial
  vehicle (UAV) capable of long-distance
  surveillance and bomb deployment
- RPG: Rocket-Propelled Grenade
  launcher

3245.98 ● ● ●

# CHAPTER THREE

# CONVICTION

"Long Shadow was supposed to be our crowning achievement," Walker explained before Cross could process the fact that *his* Shadow Squadron hadn't been the first. "They put us together to try to capture or kill Osama bin Laden."

Cross nodded. The notorious Al-Qaeda leader had eventually met his fate in a raid in Abbottabad, Pakistan. But nine years ago, he'd still been hiding out in the mountains of Afghanistan.

"It was our only job," Walker continued, "and we chased leads all over the country. Finally, we got a line on a shipment of a dialysis machine being smuggled out to a remote mining camp outside Kandahar. The theory at the time was that bin Laden had kidney failure. In light of all our other intel, we were certain we had him. So we went in to find him, but it didn't work out."

Walker stared sadly into the middle distance.

"What happened?" Cross asked.

"He wasn't there," Walker said. "We ended up flying right into an ambush. RPGs blew our bird out of the sky. Only six of us made it out of that. Three of the others died trying to complete the mission by themselves. Temple holed up in a cave and tried to lure the Taliban to him so the medic and I could get out. The medic and I played hide-and-seek with the Taliban for a week before they found us. I escaped the fight, but the medic didn't. I finally managed to make contact with Command two days later, and they sent a team in to pick me up. By the time I got home, they'd already dismantled the Shadow Squadron programme."

Walker cleared his throat and continued. "They kept the technical intelligence-gathering and psy-ops stuff intact and called it Phantom Cell. It was the direct-action side that they thought had failed so spectacularly, so they put Shadow Squadron on ice. But I suppose that after the War on Terror didn't wrap up nicely like they thought it would, Command decided to rebuild Shadow Squadron into what it is today. They fixed what they did wrong the first time around and gave it what it was missing."

"What's that?" Cross asked.

"The right leader," Walker said.

For the third time that day, Cross found himself at a loss for words. Walker flashed a small, crooked smile at him that disappeared as quickly as it had appeared. Walker nodded at Cross to let him know the sentiment was as sincere as it was difficult for the Chief to express.

Cross nodded back, grateful beyond words. "So why did Long Shadow unravel?" he asked.

"An intel leak," Howard said.

"That was the theory at the time," Walker said. "They knew we were coming. They even knew how many of us there were."

Cross nodded. "This Temple guy must've sold you out."

"Temple didn't do this," Walker said. "He wouldn't have betrayed us."

"That's him in the video, isn't it?" Cross asked. He didn't want to be cruel, but he was unwilling to ignore the obvious conclusion.

"Gareth Temple is not a traitor," Walker insisted. "I knew the man, and I never liked him, but that isn't in his nature." He pointed at the video on the whiteboard. "I don't know what that is all about, but Temple isn't a traitor. It's some kind of trick."

"Chief, I think–"

"Actually," Howard cut in, "Command's with Walker on this one, Boss."

Cross flinched. "Come again?"

"According to Phantom Cell analysts," Howard said, "tell-tale signs are all over this video." He restarted the video without sound and paused it. He used a fingertip to circle the silver calligraphy on the curtain over the scarred man's head. "You see this?

This is the bismillah. It's like a Koranic invocation of God. But the surah that these verses he quotes at the end come from – chapter nine, At-Tawba – doesn't have a bismillah."

"The verses are wrong too," Walker added. "In the first verse he quotes, he talks about the 'infidels'. The actual verse says 'Pagans'. It's making reference to a specific historical battle."

Howard gestured for Walker to continue.

"Plus it goes on after that bit about lying in wait in every stratagem of war. The verse talks about opening the way and showing mercy for any enemies who choose to accept Allah. The next verse is even more telling. It tells the reader if an enemy asks for asylum, to grant it and escort him to where he may be secure. Not something you'd tend to associate with the so-called 'sword verses' of the Koran."

"What he said," Howard said with an impressed nod.

"That last part sounded familiar too," Cross said. "Something about being the friends of God. Is that another sword verse?"

"Not exactly," Howard said. "The Phantom Cell report says it's from the speech Pope Urban the Second gave to call the First Crusade. Not exactly a standard in anti-Western jihadi rhetoric."

"But if you're some desperate, uneducated guerilla just looking to hurt somebody," Cross concluded, "it sounds like just what you'd want to hear."

"As long as you don't study your Koran too much," Walker said.

"That's also Phantom Cell's take on the video," Howard concluded. "There's a very detailed analysis of his body language, micro-expressions and a dozen other non-verbal cues here giving insight into his frame of mind. That, plus Temple's IQ, plus his mind-games expertise – it all makes a pretty good case in his favour. Mr Walker's impression is all the confirmation Command wanted. There's nobody else still alive who knew Temple well enough to give an impression of him."

Howard paused and addressed Walker for a moment. "They're still going to want you to talk to the analyst who put the profile on Temple together, of course. I suspect your gut feeling after seeing the video is going to be pretty telling, though."

"Temple was willing to give his life to save a couple of people he didn't even like," Walker said. "He's no traitor."

Cross frowned, unable to so readily accept Walker's faith in a man he'd never met. Nine years away from home in the enemy's hands could break even the strongest man. But, while Cross didn't know Temple, he did know Walker. The man's faith in his former comrade had value that couldn't be discounted.

"All right," Cross said. "What's the mission?"

"Well, as I mentioned before," Howard said, "Phantom Cell traced the video's point of origin to Shangri-La. From what they can tell, all Aswad Sayif transmissions come from there. That means it's either a base of operations or at least a central communications hub. Command plans to send an MQ-9 Reaper drone over there to blow the place apart in the near future. As for where we come in–"

"We're going in first to find out if Temple's there

and try to get him out," Cross interrupted – just in case anyone had any other ideas. Walker gave him a thankful nod.

"You got it, Boss," Carter said. "If Temple is there, we pull him out. If not, we look for evidence of his location. The problem is the Reaper's dropping its payload on schedule no matter what. We get one shot at this – and not much time to pull it off."

"That's all you'll need," Walker said, his voice full of conviction. "Bring him home, Ryan."

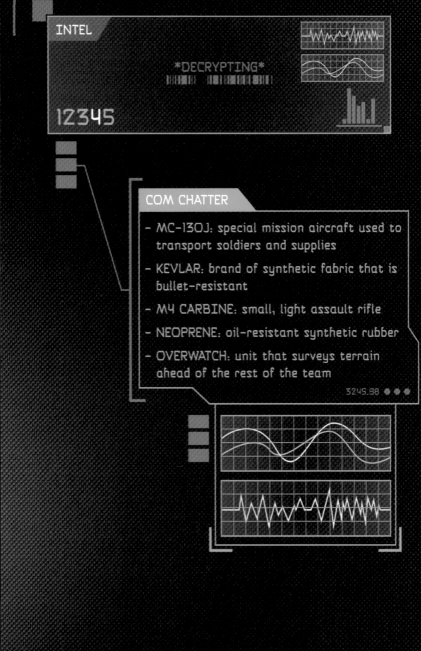

## INTEL

\*DECRYPTING\*

12345

## COM CHATTER

- MC-130J: special mission aircraft used to transport soldiers and supplies
- KEVLAR: brand of synthetic fabric that is bullet-resistant
- M4 CARBINE: small, light assault rifle
- NEOPRENE: oil-resistant synthetic rubber
- OVERWATCH: unit that surveys terrain ahead of the rest of the team

3245.98

# INFILTRATION

Two nights later, Cross arrived in Afghanistan.

After a conference with Command and a couple of long hours studying surveillance imagery of the Shangri-La target area (and the full Phantom Cell report), Cross explained the situation to the rest of the team. Then he chose Howard to go with him, as well as his team's tech expert, USAF Combat Controller Staff Sergeant Morgan Lancaster, and the medic Hospital Corpsman Second Class Kyle Williams. He needed Lancaster to coordinate the bombing run from ground level. Williams would help deal with Temple if they happened to find him unable to escape under his own power. Howard, the CIA operative, wasn't his ideal choice for a fourth man, but Command had seen fit to include him from the beginning, so Cross followed suit.

Cross left the rest of Shadow Squadron with First Sergeant Adam Paxton, a Green Beret and current second-in-command who'd taken over that role from Chief Walker. All of his soldiers had volunteered to go on the mission, but Cross felt a smaller profile best suited the situation on the ground.

Their journey took them across the sea to Base Goshta in Afghanistan's north-eastern Nangahar Province, where they had to stop for a last-minute modification to their MC-130J Commando II aircraft. Their final hop then took them over the Safed Koh mountain range where the enemy base lay hidden.

As the aircraft approached its destination, the team fell silent. Cross looked up from the touch screen of the tablet computer he'd been staring at for most of the flight. With a few taps and swipes across the screen, he sent the images he'd been studying to the other three soldiers with him. The information showed up on the tactical datapads they each wore in a Kevlar-and-neoprene bracer over the left forearm. Cross didn't like conducting ready briefings this way, but there was no central screen he could display the images on in the Commando II.

Their screens displayed a layered map of the target area. The various layers represented satellite imagery, spy drone flyover footage, a topographical projection and a more simplistic political map for perspective. Cross pulled up the topographical map on all the datapads.

"All right, listen up," Cross began. "We're minutes out from Shangri-La. This is the up-to-the-minute aerial recon of the place. Assignments haven't changed from the way I laid them out, but we're going over them again. Lancaster, I want you running overwatch and the autogun from the tree line starting here."

As Cross spoke, he tapped the spots he'd indicated on his map of the target area, highlighting the locations on the others' datapads.

"Sir," Lancaster said, not looking up from the screen on her forearm.

"Williams, Howard, you're with me," Cross said. "Howard, you'll move to the shed to disable the generators. When it's done, get back to Lancaster."

"Sure thing, Boss," Howard said.

"When he gets back," Cross said to Lancaster, "start getting the balloon ready."

"Sir."

"Williams, you'll check the stables while I check this garage out," Cross said. "I doubt Temple is in either place, but we have to rule them out. I also want to know why they need a garage when they don't have road access. Regardless, if we don't find Temple there, you and I will move into the house next. We'll search it then rendezvous with Howard and Lancaster at overwatch to catch our ride out."

"Sir," Williams replied.

With the refresher finished, Cross submitted himself to a last-minute check of his vitals from the plane's physiology tech. The scrawny kid gave him his thumbs-up and moved on to Lancaster. Cross double-checked his chute rigging and moved towards the rear of the plane. His heart raced at the expected thrill to come.

One by one, the physiology tech cleared the other three jumpers, and they all stood with Cross. He gave a signal to the tech, who passed it along by radio to the Commando II's crew. A moment later, the lights went out and the plane's rear ramp opened up. With Cross leading the way, the team descended the ramp and leapt out into the blackness over the Safed Koh mountains.

# WOOOOSH!

They opened their chutes just seconds later, still thousands of feet above the ground and miles from their target.

This technique – the high-altitude, high-opening (or HAHO) parachute jump – afforded them maximum stealth, which was crucial to this operation. The Shangri-La target site was too small and too isolated to land even the team's stealth helicopter, the Wraith. They could have landed the Wraith further away and moved in on foot, but the Reaper UAV drone bombing was scheduled to wipe Shangri-La off the map all too soon. Because that aspect of the mission was out of Cross's hands, he had to operate under that time constraint.

That meant a high jump and a swift, silent glide through the darkness. Getting in was relatively easy. Leaving was going to be the tricky bit – though Cross believed he'd settled on a trick that was up to that task.

To keep together and stay on target during the descent, the four skydivers lined up in a stack, each on top of the other. Lancaster took the lead at the bottom and directed the stack towards Shangri-La by using GPS and terrain markers. When the location was finally in sight and close enough, Lancaster gave a hand signal. The others acknowledged it, and all four broke apart again.

Lancaster angled in one direction towards her position, while Howard, Cross and Williams continued straight ahead. In minutes, they'd all touched down at their separate sites. They quickly shook off their jump rigging and buried their parachutes.

For its part, Shangri-La was beautiful in a way for a base of operations. Surrounded by grey-brown mountain tops on all sides, it lay across a triangular valley thick with lush trees. In the centre stood a two-story stone-and-stucco house that was big enough for a large family. In one corner there was a two-door garage that backed up against a set of stables big enough for two or three horses. In the second corner, the house sported an array of antennae and satellite dishes. That part was connected to a large utility shed by thick electrical cables, most likely connected to a generator within.

The third corner of the little hideaway was empty. It reminded Cross of a secretive celebrity's getaway home in the mountains. There wasn't even any indication of a road leading up to the place. There were just well-screened, well-groomed paths wide enough for a pedestrian or a nimble horse. The clearing in the corner looked just big enough to land a helicopter, though no such vehicle was visible.

Cross hunkered down. He signalled to Williams and Howard to do the same. He waited a couple of minutes before tapping the two-way canalphone in his left ear. "Overwatch, are you set?"

"Sir," Lancaster replied. "The autogun is in position. Targeting is good."

Cross tapped the *Share Screen* icon on his datapad. It showed him a feed from Lancaster's datapad, which was linked to the autogun she'd lugged along and assembled after she'd touched down. The remotely operated M110 sniper rifle sat on a heavy-duty tripod surrounded by mechanical actuators. On top of the rifle sat an extremely expensive scope with a laser range-finder, a night-vision system, a tiny Wi-Fi server, a fibre-optic camera and a host of other things Cross didn't quite understand.

Images from the scope went to Lancaster's tablet, which she could use to mark targets with a touch of a finger. The autogun could aim at and track marked targets and take them out automatically. Lancaster had argued for the use of the experimental technology for some time before Cross finally approved them. Since then, she'd proven the autogun's effectiveness repeatedly.

"Four-Eyes is up, too," Lancaster continued. "Feed's good. FLIR's good."

Four-Eyes was the team's unique quad-rotor UAV, designed by Lancaster's predecessor on the team. The drone was decked out with mini-cameras, forward-looking infrared (FLIR) sensors, a range-finder, shotgun microphones and even a PA speaker. Four-Eyes was a nearly invisible reconnaissance and spying tool. It was able to transmit a feed to the other soldiers' tactical datapads at a touch as well.

"Roger that," Cross said, confirming the infrared feed on his datapad. He looked at Howard and Williams and pointed towards their separate objectives. They nodded and split off towards the stable and the utility shed.

Cross pulled a glare shield down over his datapad, flipped down his monocular night vision system, and began moving towards the concrete garage.

"No heat signatures from the shed," Lancaster reported. "Two in the stables, one in the garage."

"Stables confirmed," Williams said. "Two insurgent horses. Otherwise clear."

Cross's mouth twitched in a brief grin. "What about the shed?"

"I'm in," Howard reported. "It's clear. Eyes on the generator."

"Work your magic," Cross said.

Moving through the tree cover and underbrush as quietly as possible, Cross headed towards the garage. It had two single-panel doors on the front, though no car-sized path led up to it. With no way to get a car anywhere near to it, Cross wondered exactly what the building was actually used for.

He crept to a wooden door around the corner and slowly, very slowly, turned the handle. It wasn't locked, and it turned silently. Cross opened the door a sliver and peeked inside. An Afghani in his early twenties was reading a book with his back to the door. An AK-47 automatic rifle was propped up next to the chair he was sitting on.

"This should do it," Howard said. "In three, two, one…"

# WHIRRRRRRR…

As Howard ended his count, a horrific grinding noise came from the utility shed, followed by a whoosh of blue-grey smoke. Whatever Howard had done had knocked the generator out of commission. Every light in the house and the garage went out, plunging the entire area into darkness. From inside the house, Cross heard a commotion and annoyed voices raised in confusion.

When darkness fell, Cross slipped inside the garage, raised his M4 carbine over his head and brought it down hard over the seated sentry's skull.

# THUD.

The target was pawing around for his rifle when the butt of Cross's M4 knocked him out cold. Cross eased him to the floor and slid the magazine out of the AK-47.

With that done, he looked around to see what the man had been guarding. As he scanned the walls, he could barely believe his eyes.

"Clear," Cross reported distractedly.

"I'm out," Howard reported, sounding supremely pleased with himself.

"You're clear to the trees," Lancaster reported.

"On my way to you, Commander," Williams said.

When the medic arrived at Cross's position, he took one look around and saw what Cross had seen. "Sheesh," he said, barely above a whisper.

"Can you believe it?" Cross whispered back.

The garage was packed to the rafters with racks of assault rifles, metal ammo boxes and firearms.

But most disturbing of all were the crates upon crates of high-incendiary thermite grenades. Cross had hoped this relatively isolated building might be where Temple was being held. Instead, they'd stumbled upon what seemed to be an insurgent weapons cache – and a rather large one at that.

Cross softly relayed the information to Lancaster, who then passed that information along to the Reaper's remote pilot for when the drone started its attack run. She also pointed out that the deadline for that event was quickly approaching.

"Noted," Cross said, tapping his canalphone. As he spoke, he and Williams left the garage and headed towards the house. Between them and the back door lay a well-kept poppy garden. The poppy bulbs were all closed, giving the strange garden the surreal impression of dozens of tiny fists raised in defiance.

"Two people coming out just ahead of you," Lancaster reported as Cross and Williams drew close.

Cross raised his hand to halt Williams. They both flattened themselves against the wall around the corner just in time to avoid the men that Four-Eyes' FLIR camera had spotted. One of the men held a torch and was strapping a rifle over his shoulder with his free hand. The other man carried a toolbox and was chattering breathlessly in Pashto. As they approached the shed, they left the back door open.

"One more moving around downstairs in the room on the south-facing wall," Lancaster said. "Three signatures upstairs, all prone. They're probably sleeping."

Cross tapped his canalphone to acknowledge

and motioned Williams to follow him into the house. They entered through the open front door, gliding through the inky black interior like ghosts. The house was small but nicely decorated.

From the open kitchen, they saw an Afghani man fumbling through drawers and cabinets, probably looking for matches or another torch. Though they passed by him no more than two metres away, he didn't hear or see them. Trusting in their night-vision equipment and in Howard's thorough disabling of the generator, they made their way upstairs.

The house's top floor consisted of five rooms off a long, straight corridor. They moved as quickly as they could, peeking into each room as they went. The first room was empty. The next two contained sleeping men that Cross and Williams didn't recognize. The fourth was a sparse room with a blood-red desk in the middle, a digital camera on one side and a black curtain with silvery Arabic letters painted on it. Cross recognized it at once, but Temple wasn't there. Cross cautiously made his way to the last room at the far end of the corridor.

The last room was the largest and the nicest. A lush, four-poster bed dominated it. On it lay Gareth Temple, sprawled on his back and snoring through what sounded like a painfully blocked nose. He twitched and writhed weakly in his sleep. His legs fidgeted on the bed every now and again. He stunk of body odour, and his sheets were clammy with sweat.

In these surroundings, Temple didn't look like a prisoner, but he certainly wasn't at peace. Frowning, Cross gestured for Williams to come over to Temple's bed. The medic planted a boot softly on the bed, propped his M4 on his knee to steady it, then bent over and covered Temple's mouth with one gloved hand. Temple flinched and his eyes flew open. He tried to struggle, but his hands were trapped in his sheet and he was clearly weak and disoriented.

Cross pulled the glare shield down off his tactical datapad and brought the device to life. He tapped an icon to bring up a message he'd written earlier, then turned the bracer around so Temple could see it.

*Temple,* it read. *Keep quiet and don't panic.*

## INTEL

*DECRYPTING*

12345

## COM CHATTER

- CARABINER: ring with a spring catch used as an attachment to rope
- EXFILTRATION: quietly and sneakily escaping from an area under enemy control
- OP: short for operation, or a mission
- PROSTHETIC: a device used to compensate for an individual's missing limb or body part

3245.98 ● ● ●

# CHAPTER FIVE

# EXFILTRATION

On the bed, Temple froze. His eyes darted back and forth in their sunken sockets. The soft glow from the datapad screen cast his pale skin and waxy burn scar in sickly green light. He stopped resisting and nodded slowly. Williams uncovered the man's mouth but kept his M4 trained on him.

Temple sat up very slowly, peering back and forth from Cross to Williams in child-like fear. "Who are you?" he whispered.

Cross tapped his datapad again, bringing up a second message he'd prepared in advance for such a question.

*Shadow Squadron,* it read.

Reading those words, something inside Temple snapped. He shuddered, and tears welled up in his eyes. He half collapsed against Williams' leg and clung to it like a drowning man. No sound emerged from him, but his whole body heaved in silent sobs as tears rolled down both cheeks.

Williams freed himself as carefully as he could, then he and Cross helped Temple out of the bed. They pulled a jacket over his stick-thin, trembling arms and helped him get a slipper onto his right foot and a wooden prosthetic boot over the end of his left leg. Then they ushered him towards the door. Though he could stand and support himself, he continued to cling to Williams as if he couldn't believe the situation was real.

Cross replaced the glare shield over his datapad and tapped his canalphone twice to let Lancaster and Howard know he was on his way out.

"The first two guys are still in the shed," Lancaster informed him. "The third guy's got a torch, and he's checking on the horses. He's armed too, but you're clear if you hurry. The Commando II's on its way. The Reaper's right behind it."

Cross and Williams nodded to each other and hustled Temple out of the door, down the corridor and to the stairs. They made it about halfway to the first floor when Temple suddenly grabbed the banister and froze in place, his eyes shut tight. He took a deep, raggedy breath before he opened his eyes again.

"Dizzy," he whispered. Greasy sweat shone on his forehead. "But I'm okay."

They started again, but it was slower going now. Temple's initial rush of energy had drained away, and his legs were wobbly. Williams had to sling his M4 over his shoulder and use both arms to support Temple through the rest of the house to the back door. Cross had just placed a hand on the door handle when Temple stumbled.

Williams began to lift Temple up into a fireman's carry, but Temple shook his head violently. "I can make it," he insisted in a heated whisper.

Cross decided to give him one more chance and turned back to the door. He'd just turned the handle when Lancaster suddenly hissed in his canalphone. "Stop, stop! They're coming back."

Cross peeked out to see two men with torches and a third carrying a toolbox just outside the shed. The men with torches also had AK-47s slung across their backs. All three of them talked rapidly for a few seconds, gesticulating at the shed and the house and each other.

None of them knew what was going on, but if Cross tried to open the door in plain sight of them, they'd work it out pretty quickly. His hand tightened on his M4. He couldn't afford to wait more than a few seconds. If they missed their plane, they were going to be at ground zero when the Reaper turned this whole place into rubble.

"Hold tight," Lancaster said. "I've got you."

Before Cross could ask what she meant, he heard the familiar hum of Four-Eyes' four internal rotors as the small UAV dropped down dangerously close to ground level in front of the garage.

The machine was ultra-quiet, but when Lancaster moved it in close enough, the Afghanis heard it even if they couldn't identify it. They waved their torches towards the sound, but Lancaster had already moved the UAV over their heads. She brought it down low again over the top of the shed and then behind it.

## TAP. TAP. TAP.

Ever so carefully, Lancaster bumped Four-Eyes into the back of the shed a couple of times. The three Afghanis hurried around to the back of the shed to determine the source of the noise. As soon as their backs were turned, Lancaster simply said, "Go."

Cross and Williams didn't need to be told – they were already out of the door, supporting Temple between them. They darted around to the side of the house and hurried towards the tree line where Lancaster and Howard were waiting. As they made it to cover, Lancaster launched Four-Eyes up and out, leaving the Afghanis scratching their heads and staring at nothing.

"We're clear," Cross whispered with a tap on his canalphone. A moment later, he caught a flash in the distance from the screen of Howard's tactical datapad that shone brightly in his night-vision. Cross, Williams and Temple used the brief flash as a guide and met up with the others at overwatch.

Lancaster was packing Four-Eyes away and shouldering her rucksack. Howard was uncoiling a heavy-duty line from around his shoulders and clipping a carabiner at the end to a handle on the autogun. The other end disappeared into a bag Lancaster had brought with her. More carabiners were tied onto the line at long, regular intervals – five in all.

"This is the wrong way," Temple wheezed, out of breath and wavering on his feet. He looked like he might topple any second. "The path is on the north side. There's no way down on this side."

"We're not going down," Cross said. He and the other three soldiers were clipping carabiners from the line into harnesses over their chests. He gave Williams a nod, and the medic dug a matching fifth harness out of Howard's pack and helped Temple wriggle into it.

"You can't land a helicopter here," Temple said, his eyes widening in growing panic. "They'll blow it out of the sky. They'll think I called you. You don't know what they'll do. You have no idea what they'll do to us!"

"We don't need a helicopter," Cross said.

Williams had tightened Temple's harness as best

he could, and Cross clipped the last carabiner from the heavy-duty line to it. In the distance, they could hear the roar of MC-130J's engines approaching. The plane was moving fast and coming in low.

"They'll hear," Temple moaned. "They're going to realize I've gone…"

"Relax," Cross said. "We're leaving."

Cross looked at Lancaster. She nodded and dug a basketball-sized object out of the pack on the ground. It was black and featureless except for a metallic handle attached to a ripcord. It was also attached to the top of the line. Lancaster gave a last visual inspection of the rigging that bound them all together. Then she pulled the ripcord.

# TSSSSSSSSS.

The object in her hands hissed, and she threw it into the air. To Temple's obvious astonishment, the device revealed itself to be a silvery-white weather balloon on a rapid air inflator. It swelled instantly to its full size and shot up into the air, rising metres above the tops of the tallest trees. A white light dangled beneath it, as well as an infrared beacon.

"You must be joking," Temple gasped, recognizing what was about to happen. "Nobody does this anymore."

"Classics never go out of style," Cross said with a grin.

Temple wasn't wrong, though. The technique Cross had chosen for their escape hadn't been used much, if at all, in almost twenty years.

Voices rose in alarm from the house as the Afghanis noticed the impossible-to-miss balloon rising from the forest. They shouted to wake the others in the house, which only gave rise to more shouting and confusion. That sound was soon dwarfed by the roar of the approaching Commando II's engines.

"Allahu Akbar," Temple chanted, sending himself into a near-trance. "Allahu Akbar. Allahu Akbar. Allahu Akbar..."

As the men from the house came pounding

through the trees to investigate, Shadow Squadron's MC-130J appeared from over the top of a nearby mountain and swooped low over the tree line. Homing in on the weather balloon's flashing light and IR beacon, the pilot managed to get the plane's nose just under the balloon before he had to pull up on the stick to pull out of the valley.

The V-shaped yoke Cross had added to the plane's nose at Goshta snagged the heavy-duty line trailing from the balloon and locked it in place.

## SWOOOOSH!

With all the might of the Commando II's engines above them, the five Shadow Squadron soldiers, new and old, were gracefully lifted into the sky. The last thing to leave the ground was Lancaster's autogun trailing from the end of the line.

The only item they left behind was Temple's prosthetic boot, which fell off as he left the ground.

This technique was called the Fulton surface-to-

air recovery system, but Cross strongly preferred it's nickname: Skyhook. It had been developed in the 1950s for the CIA, and the US special forces adopted it for airlifting people and cargo in a hurry from dangerous places.

The system hadn't been used much since newer and better helicopters were developed, but it was still well suited to a few rare situations. Cross had felt that this was just such a situation. And besides, the twelve year old in him had always wanted to try it.

In this case, Skyhook had proven to be a great success – and not a moment too soon, either. Just moments after the winch began to reel everyone up, Cross heard a second plane's engine noise overlap their own plane's output. He didn't see the Reaper drone coming, but he heard it when its payload of four AGM-114 Hellfire missiles detonated.

# KRAKA-BOOM.
# BOOM-BOOM-BOOM!

With his night-vision lens flipped up, he saw two missiles hit the house. One decimated the garage. The fourth missile went wide and came down in the trees awfully close to where Lancaster had set up her overwatch position. In seconds, the entire hidden valley was on fire, wiping the area off the map.

\* \* \*

Some hours later, their plane flew just ahead of the rising sun. "Temple's out cold," Williams told Cross. "It's best we let him sleep for a while."

"What's his condition?" Cross asked.

"He's sick. He's got a severe morphine addiction. Probably goes all the way back to when he was captured. I gave him a dose to get him home, but withdrawal's going to be nasty. Otherwise, he's physically fine. He's got a lot of old burn scars, and he's missing half his leg and an ear, but they did a decent job of keeping him alive."

"Stay with him," Cross said.

Williams nodded and went back to Temple's side.

Howard was sitting next to Lancaster, helping

her disassemble and pack away the autogun. Cross caught his eye and nodded for the CIA man to come over. Howard left Lancaster to join Cross by the closed cargo ramp.

"You heard his story," Cross said in low tones.

As soon as they were safely on the plane, Temple had breathlessly given them all a horrific account of what had happened immediately after the disastrous *Operation: Long Shadow*. After forcing Walker and the team's medic to leave him, he'd fired a shot from his pistol to draw the Taliban hunters' attention only to discover that the gun had had only one bullet in it. Unable to resist, he'd been captured. Although the immediate aftermath of that capture had been blurry to him, he'd found himself alive and patched up – only to undergo a terrible odyssey of torture and psychological manipulation that made Cross shudder.

"The stuff of nightmares," Howard said. "I can't believe he's made it through all that."

"He's made it through by converting to Islam and collaborating with the enemy," Cross said matter-of-factly. "He agreed to become the public face of Aswad Sayif. Some people back home are going to say he gave aid and comfort to the enemy."

"Some are," Howard said. The sour look on his face made clear his opinion of such people. "But they tortured him, hooked him on drugs and kept him prisoner for almost ten years. He did what he had to do to survive."

"Yes, he did," Cross said. "I just hope he realizes the nightmare's not over yet. It might never be."

Howard frowned. He peered at Cross. "Is this what you wanted to talk to me about, Boss?"

"No," Cross admitted. "I wanted to talk about *Long Shadow*. Walker said there was a leak that blew the op. And then before I'd ever heard about it, Command came to you."

"With questions," Howard said.

"Because you used to work for Upton," Cross said. "Yes?"

Howard nodded.

"Was he involved in *Long Shadow*?" Cross asked.

Howard nodded again. "Just before they sent him to Iraq. That's why they sent him to Iraq – it was his mission and it flopped badly. It was a stain on his career. I met him after all that happened, though."

"But *Long Shadow* didn't just flop," Cross said. "Upton blew the op on purpose."

"That's what Command thinks," Howard said. "That's why they came to me with their questions first. He'd mentioned *Long Shadow* when I knew him, but he had never told me anything specific about it. That's what I told Command. Then they told me about Temple and asked me to get you and Walker in to see the video. I wanted to let you know what was going on up front, but they told me not to until you got back to base."

"I understand," Cross said. "No harm done."

"If you say so, Boss," Howard said. "Now if you don't have anything else for me, I think I need some sleep. It's been a long night."

Cross nodded. *Longer for some than others,* he thought.

## MISSION DEBRIEFING

OPERATION

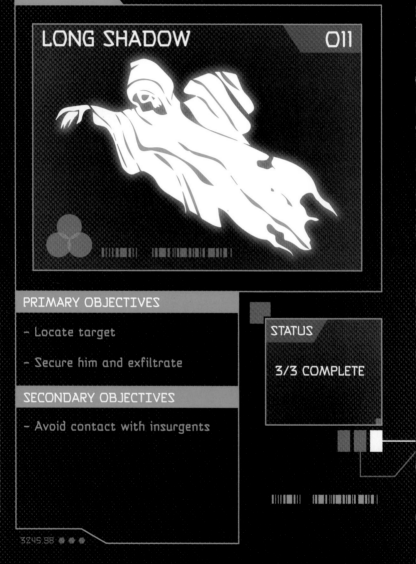

### LONG SHADOW

O11

### PRIMARY OBJECTIVES

- Locate target

- Secure him and exfiltrate

### SECONDARY OBJECTIVES

- Avoid contact with insurgents

STATUS

3/3 COMPLETE

3245.98 ● ● ●

# CROSS, RYAN

RANK: Lieutenant Commander
BRANCH: Navy Seal
PSYCH PROFILE: Team leader
of Shadow Squadron. Control
oriented and loyal, Cross insisted
on hand-picking each member of
his squad.

This mission was nearly perfect. Howard and Lancaster and Williams deserve praise for their efforts. Lancaster especially demonstrated creativity in the field and probably saved all our lives with her UAV stunt.

And most importantly, we recovered our target and exfiltrated without issue. While Temple's ordeal is far from over, at least he's safe now. Job well done, team.

– Lieutenant Commander Ryan Cross

## *ERROR*

### UNAUTHORIZED

USER MUST HAVE LEVEL 12 CLEARANCE
OR HIGHER IN ORDER TO GAIN ACCESS
TO FURTHER MISSION INFORMATION.

2019.681

# CLASSIFIED

## CREATOR BIO(S)

### AUTHOR

# CARL BOWEN

Carl Bowen is a father, husband, and writer living in Georgia, USA. He was born in Louisiana, lived briefly in England, and was raised in Georgia where he went to school. He has published a handful of novels, short stories, and comics, including retellings of *20,000 Leagues Under the Sea*, *The Strange Case of Dr. Jekyll and Mr. Hyde*, *The Jungle Book*, *Aladdin and the Magic Lamp*, *Julius Caesar* and *The Murders in the Rue Morgue*. He is the original author of *BMX Breakthrough* as well as the Shadow Squadron series.

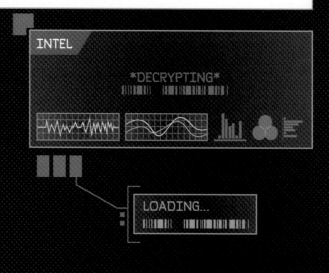

# WILSON TORTOSA

Wilson "Wunan" Tortosa is a Filipino comic book artist best known for his work on *Tomb Raider* and the American relaunch of *Battle of the Planets* for Top Cow Productions. Wilson attended Philippine Cultural High School, then went on to the University of Santo Tomas where he graduated with a degree in Fine Arts.

# BENNY FUENTES

Benny Fuentes lives in Tabasco, Mexico, where the temperature is just as hot as the sauce. He studied graphic design in college, but now he works as a full-time illustrator in the comic book and graphic novel industry for companies like Marvel, DC Comics and Top Cow Productions. He shares his home with two crazy cats, Chelo and Kitty, who act like they own the place.

2019.681

# CLASSIFIED

## AUTHOR DEBRIEFING

### CARL BOWEN

Q/When and why did you decide to become a writer?

A/I've enjoyed writing ever since I was at primary school. I wrote as much as I could, hoping to become the next Lloyd Alexander or Stephen King, but I didn't sell my first story until I was at university. It had been a long wait, but the day I saw my story in print was one of the best days of my life.

Q/What made you decide to write *Shadow Squadron*?

A/As a child, my heroes were always brave knights or noble loners who fought because it was their duty, not for fame or glory. I think the special ops soldiers of the US military embody those ideals. Their jobs are difficult and often thankless, so I wanted to show how cool their jobs are and also express my gratitude for our brave warriors.

Q/What inspires you to write?

A/My biggest inspiration is my family. My wife's love and support lifts me up when this job seems too hard to keep going. My son is another big inspiration.

He's three years old, and I want him to read my books and feel the same way I did when I read my favourite books as a child. And if he happens to grow up to become an elite soldier in the US military, that would be pretty awesome, too.

Q/Describe what it was like to write these books.
A/The only military experience I have is a year I spent in the Army ROTC. It gave me a great respect for the military and its soldiers, but I quickly realized I would have made an awful soldier. I recently got to test out some firearms for research on this book. I got to blow apart an old fax machine.

Q/What is your favourite book, film and game?
A/My favourite book of all time is *Don Quixote*. It's crazy and it makes me laugh. My favourite film is either *Casablanca* or *Double Indemnity*, old black-and-white films made before I was born. My favourite game, hands down, is *Skyrim*, in which you play a heroic dragonslayer. But not even *Skyrim* can keep me from writing more *Shadow Squadron* stories, so you won't have to wait long to read more about Ryan Cross and his team. That's a promise.

INTEL

*DECRYPTING*

ALPHA

## COM CHATTER

-MISSION PREVIEW: After an unknown aircraft crashes in Antarctica near a science facility, Shadow Squadron is deployed to recover the device. But when Russian special forces intervene, Cross gets caught between the mission's objective and the civilian scientists' safety.

3245.98 ● ● ●

SHADOW SQUADRON

PHANTOM SUN

CARL BOWEN

# PHANTOM SUN

Cross tapped his touch screen to start the video. On the screen, a few geologists began pointing and waving frantically. The camera watched them all for another couple of seconds then lurched around in a semicircle and tilted skywards. Blurry clouds wavered in and out of focus for a second before the cameraman found what the others had been pointing at – a lance of white fire in the sky. The image focused, showing what appeared to be a meteorite with a trailing white plume behind it punching through a hole in the clouds. The camera zoomed out to allow the cameraman to better track the object's progress through the sky.

"Is that a meteorite?" Shepherd asked.

"Just keep watching," Brighton said, breathless with anticipation.

Right on cue, the supposed meteorite suddenly flared white, then changed direction in mid-flight by almost 45 degrees. Grunts and hisses of surprise filled the room.

"So … not a meteorite," Shepherd muttered.

The members of Shadow Squadron watched as the falling object changed direction once again with another flare and then pitched downwards. The camera angle twisted overhead and then lowered to track its earthward trajectory from below.

"And now … sonic boom," Brighton said.

The camera image shook violently for a second as the compression wave from the falling object broke the speed of sound and as the accompanying burst shook the cameraman's hands. A moment later, the object streaked into the distance and disappeared into the rolling hills of ice and snow. The video footage ended a few moments later with a still image of the

gawking geologists looking as excited as children on Christmas morning.

"This video popped up on the internet a few hours ago," Cross began. "It's already started to go viral."

"What is it?" Second Lieutenant Aram Jannati said. Jannati, the team's newest member, came from the Marine Special Operations Regiment. "I can't imagine we'd get involved if it was just a meteor."

"Meteorite," Staff Sergeant Adam Paxton corrected. "If it gets through the atmosphere to the ground, it's a meteorite."

"That wasn't a meteorite, man," Brighton said, hopping out of his chair. He dug his smartphone out of a pocket and walked around the table towards the front of the room. He laid his phone on the touch screen Cross had used, and then synced up the two devices. With that done, he used his phone as a remote control to run the video backwards to the first time the object had changed directions. He used a slider to move the timer back and forth, showing the object's fairly sharp angle of deflection through the sky.

"Meteorites can't change direction like this," Brighton said. "This is 45 degrees of deflection at least, and it barely even slows down."

"I'm seeing a flare when it turns," Paxton said. "Meteors hold a lot of frozen water when they're in space. It expands when it reaches the atmosphere. If those gases are venting or exploding, couldn't that cause a change of direction?"

"Not this sharply," Brighton said before Cross could reply. "Besides, if you look at this…" He used a few swipes across his phone to pause the video and zoom in on the flying object. At the new resolution, a dark, oblong shape was visible inside a wreath of fire. He then advanced through the first and second changes of direction and tracked it a few seconds forward before pausing again. "See?"

A room full of shrugs and uncomprehending looks met Brighton's eager gaze.

"It's the same size!" Brighton said, throwing his hands up in mock frustration. "If this thing had exploded twice – and with enough force to push something this big in a different direction both times – it would be in a million pieces. So those aren't explosions. They're thrusters or something."

"Which makes this what?" Shepherd asked. "A UFO?"

"Sure," Paxton answered in a mocking tone. "It's unidentified, it's flying and it's surely an object. It probably has little green men inside, too."

"You don't know that it doesn't," Brighton said. "I mean, it could be from outer space!"

"Sit down, Sergeant," Chief Walker said.

Brighton reluctantly did so, pocketing his phone.

"Don't get ahead of yourself, Ed," Cross said, retaking control of the briefing. "Phantom Cell analysts have authenticated the video and concluded that this thing isn't just a meteorite. It's some sort of metal construct, though they can't make out specifics from the quality of the video. I suppose it's possible it's from outer space, but it's much more likely to be man-made. All we know for certain is that it's not American made. Therefore, our mission is to get out to where it came down, secure it, zip it up and bring it back for a full analysis. Any questions so far?"

"I have one," Jannati said. "What is Phantom Cell?"

Cross nodded. Jannati was the newest member of the team, and as such he wasn't as familiar with all the various secret programmes. "Phantom Cell is a parallel programme to ours," Cross explained. "But their focus is on psy-ops, cyberwarfare and research and development."

Jannati nodded. "Geeks, in other words," he said. Brighton gave him a sour look but said nothing.

"What are we supposed to do about the scientists who found this thing?" Lieutenant Kimiyo Yamashita asked. True to his stoic nature, the sniper had finished his breakfast and coffee while everyone else was talking excitedly. "Do they know we're coming?"

"That's the problem," Cross said, frowning. "We haven't heard a peep out of them since this video appeared online. Attempts to contact them have gone unanswered. The last anyone heard, the geologists who made the video were going to try to find the point of impact where this object came down. We have no idea whether they found it or not, or what happened to them."

"Isn't this how the film *Aliens* started?" Brighton asked. "With a space colony suddenly cutting off communication after a UFO crash landing?"

Paxton rolled his eyes. "Lost Aspen, the base there, is pretty new," he said. "And it's in the middle of Antarctica. It could just be a simple technical failure."

"You have no imagination, man," Brighton said. "You're going to be the first one the monster eats. Well … after me, anyway."

"These are our orders," Cross continued as if he hadn't been interrupted. "Find what crashed, bring the object back for study, work out why the research station stopped communicating and make sure the civilians are safe. Stealth is going to be of paramount importance here. Nobody has any territorial claims on Marie Byrd Land, but no country is supposed to be sending troops on missions anywhere in Antarctica, either."

"Are we expecting anyone else to be breaking that rule while we are, Commander?" Yamashita asked.

"It's possible," Cross said. "If this object is man-made, whoever made it is probably going to come looking for it. Any other government that attached the same significance to the video that ours did could send people, too. No specific intel has been confirmed yet, but it's only a matter of time before someone takes an active interest."

"Seems like the longer the video's out there, the more likely we're going to have company," Yamashita said.

"About that," Cross said with a mischievous smile on his face. "Phantom Cell's running a psy-ops campaign in support of our efforts. They're simultaneously spreading the word that the video's a hoax and doing their best to stop it from spreading and to remove it from circulation."

"Good luck to them on that last one," Brighton snorted. "It's the internet. Phantom Cell's good, but nobody's that good."

"Not our concern," Cross said. "We ship out in one hour. Get your equipment onto the Commando. We'll go over more mission specifics during the flight. Understood?"

"Sir," the men responded in unison. At a nod from Cross, they rose and gathered up the remains of their breakfast. As they left the briefing room, Walker remained behind. He gulped down the last of his coffee before standing up.

"Brighton's certainly excited," Walker said.

"I knew he would be," Cross replied. "I didn't expect him to try to help out so much with the briefing, though."

"Is that what I'm like whenever I chip in from up here?" Walker asked.

Cross fought off the immediate urge to toy with his second-in-command, though he couldn't stop the mischievous smile from coming back. "Maybe a little bit," he said.

Walker returned Cross's grin. "Then I wholeheartedly apologize."

*TRANSMISSION ERROR*

PLEASE CONTACT YOUR LOCAL LIBRARY OR BOOKSELLER FOR MORE DETAILS...

LOGGING OUT...

2012.101